This book belongs to

....

LADYBIRD BOOKS

UK | USA | Canada | Ireland | Australia | India | New Zealand | South Africa

Ladybird Books is part of the Penguin Random House group of companies
whose addresses can be found at global.penguinrandomhouse.com.

www.penguin.co.uk   www.puffin.co.uk   www.ladybird.co.uk

Penguin
Random House
UK

First published 2022
001

Licensed by

Printed in China

The authorized representative in the EEA is Penguin Random House Ireland,
Morrison Chambers, 32 Nassau Street, Dublin D02 YH68

A CIP catalogue record for this book is available from the British Library

ISBN: 978-0-241-57567-3

All correspondence to:
Ladybird Books, Penguin Random House Children's
One Embassy Gardens, 8 Viaduct Gardens, London SW11 7BW

Peppa's Dragon Adventure

It was night-time, and Peppa and George were ready for bed. Peppa climbed the ladder up to her bunk bed, but George wouldn't get into his.

"What's the matter, George?" asked Daddy Pig. "Don't you want to go to bed?"

George shook his head.
"George doesn't want to have a **bad dream**," explained Peppa, "so he doesn't want to go to bed."

"I'm sure we can fix that with a good bedtime story," said
Daddy Pig. "Snuggle down, and I'll begin . . ."

"Once upon a time, there was a grand castle high up in the sky. It was home to a very special family . . . Queen Mummy, King Daddy, Princess Peppa and Prince George."

"That's us!" Peppa whispered to George.
George giggled. "Hee! Hee! Hee!"

"The family did lots of important things together," said Daddy Pig. "Didn't they, Mummy Pig?"
"Oh, yes," said Mummy Pig. "Important things like . . .

"sitting on their comfy thrones . . .

"eating delicious food . . .

"and reading bedtime stories in their cosy royal beds."

"And playing hide-and-seek!" said Peppa.
"Yes, and playing hide-and-seek,"
agreed Mummy Pig.

"One day, when they were playing a game of hide-and-seek," continued Mummy Pig, "Prince George spotted something sparkly." "It was . . . an egg," said Daddy Pig. "A giant golden egg . . .

"Prince George thought it was a chocolate egg,
wrapped in golden foil.
'Yummy!' cried Prince George, going to take a bite . . .
CLUNK! It wasn't chocolate, it was
made of **real gold!**"

CLUNK!

"Suddenly," said Mummy Pig, "Prince George heard Princess Peppa singing, *'I'm coming to find you, Prince George!'*

"When Princess Peppa found him, he showed her the golden egg. 'Ooooh. How fancy!' she said.

"Prince George showed it to the queen and king. 'Ooooh. How fancy!' they said.

"Queen Mummy put the egg where everyone could see it. 'Thank you, Prince George,' she said. 'Doesn't it look lovely?'"

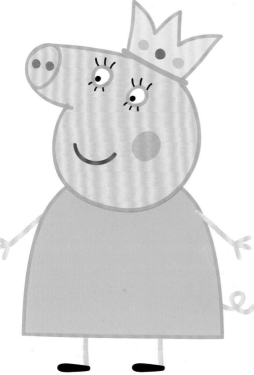

"Great ending, Mummy Pig," said Daddy Pig. "Are you ready to go to bed now, George?"

"No," said George, shaking his head.

"I know," said Peppa. "I'll do a bit more story . . ."

Yaay!

"The next day," began Peppa, "the family saw
that the giant golden egg . . . had hatched!
'Oh no!' everyone cried."

"So the family went on a hunt for . . ."

"Dine-saw. *Grrr!*" cheered George.

"Hee! Hee! Funny George, it wasn't a dinosaur," said Peppa.

"The family searched the whole castle, but couldn't find anything!

"Princess Peppa had an idea. 'Let's look in the garden.'
The prince and princess ran outside, where they spotted a line
of huge footprints on the royal lawn. 'Follow that trail!' cried
Princess Peppa."

"They followed the footprints into the forest," continued Peppa, "where they discovered . . . a **huge** dragon with **massive** wings!

"The dragon picked up the prince and the princess, put them on her back and took them on a magical flight! They soared over mountains and flew higher than the clouds . . . until it was finally time for the dragon to deliver them to their royal beds. The end!" said Peppa.

Yawn!

"Now are you ready to get into bed, George?" asked Peppa.
"Yes," said George.
"I'm sure, after all that adventure, you'll have lovely dreams,"
said Mummy Pig.

"And, if anything happens in your dream that you don't like, George," said Peppa, "I will come riding in on our dragon and save you!"

"Yay! Drag-on!" cheered George.

Peppa and George soon fell fast asleep . . .

George dreamed he was riding a
magnificent dragon and flying high
above the clouds with Peppa. It was
the best dream ever!

The next morning, George woke up excited.
"Drag-on!" he shouted.
Peppa told Mummy and Daddy Pig that George
loved the dragon story so much, he wanted to find
a real dragon.
"That's lovely, George," said Mummy Pig,
"but dragons aren't real, I'm afraid."

"Some are real, aren't they, Mummy?"
asked Peppa.
Before Mummy Pig could answer,
there was a flash of something green
outside the kitchen window.

"DRAG-ON!" cheered George.

"Really?" said Daddy Pig, looking up.

George nodded.

"Right, well maybe we should go and check?" said Daddy Pig.

"Hooray!" cheered Peppa. "Another dragon hunt!"

Peppa, George, Mummy and Daddy Pig headed off in search of the dragon. They soon spotted some tracks in the forest. "Follow that trail!" cried Peppa.

The tracks led all the way to a castle.
"DRAG-ON!" cheered George, looking up and seeing
Miss Rabbit on top of a huge **robot dragon!**
"Oh my, it *is* a dragon!" said Mummy Pig.

"This is my robot dragon!" Miss Rabbit shouted down.
"Sometimes I use it as part of the tour at the castle!
Would you like to give it a go?"

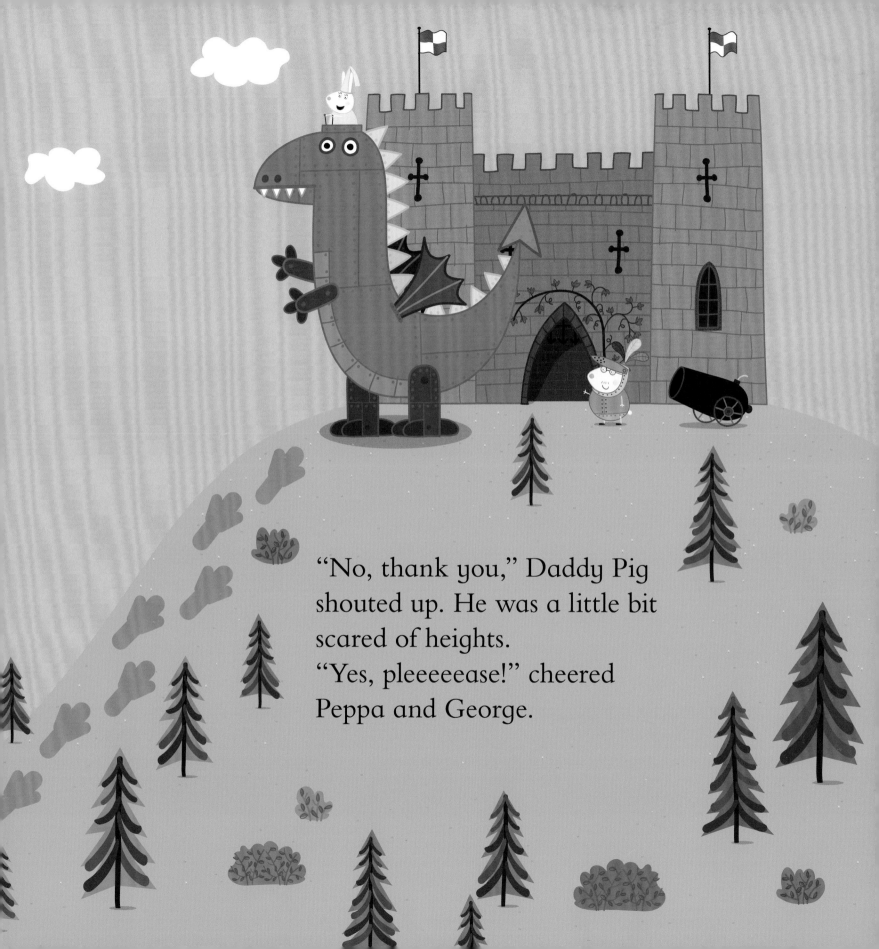

"No, thank you," Daddy Pig
shouted up. He was a little bit
scared of heights.
"Yes, pleeeeease!" cheered
Peppa and George.

Miss Rabbit gave Peppa and
George a ride on the robot dragon.
They were so high, their heads
were up in the clouds!
"George!" cried Peppa.
"Isn't riding a dragon
magical? Just like our story!"
"Yaaaaay!" cried
George. "Drag-on!"

Yaaaaay!

After the ride was over, Miss Rabbit gave Peppa and George toy dragons from the souvenir shop to take home.
"Drag-on! *ROAR!*" said George happily.

That night, Peppa and George cuddled their toy dragons in bed, and they both fell fast asleep . . . even before Mummy and Daddy Pig could finish their bedtime story!
"I'm sure after that dragon adventure, they'll sleep really well!" said Daddy Pig.

Peppa and George love dragons.
Everyone loves dragons!